PAY

ATTENTION

Pat Brown

By Downtown Pat Brown

Creative Direction: Patricia E. Brown, Tamiko Lowry Pugh,
Bernadine C. Taylor

Edited by Brown & Taylor Associates Literary Services

Published by Still Standing Publishing Company

Photographs, Courtesy of Patricia E. Brown and Peaches Photography

Printed in the United States of America

ISBN: 9798617748101

<u>Dedicated to my children</u>

Bernard, Kenneth, Cynthia, (In Memoriam)

Judith, Colvina, Nadine,

Gloria, Bernadine & Michael

And to all of my

Grand, Great Grand and Great Great

GRAND CHILDREN!

"MY TRIBE"

MANY THANKS

To all of my family and friends

Thanks for your love and support!

Foreword

Mother indeed learned obedience, *much like Christ*, by the things *she suffered.* And it is not only an honor but a privilege to be an integral part of this awesome feat as we prepared to give *you* what she gives to the world; through her wit, ingenuity, and charisma. It took many hours of talking on the phone, visiting and jotting down notes, in her living room *and* several years of driving throughout the *City of Buffalo, New York,* listening to her poignant description of great old (*Downtown*) landmarks and grim reminders of '*what it meant*' and '*what it took*' to become a proud young brown girl who grew up shortly after the *Great Depression.* Depicted by her clear-cut antidoted styled chapters, she is no joke! "*Pay Attention's*" contents consist of wisdom nuggets which is also depicted by much of a *Southern* drawl (*dialect*) that she inherited from her *Grandparents,* who migrated from the *South* to the *North.* Notwithstanding, on each visit, Mother would give me *fifty-year old documents* that resembled papers as if they were only *a few weeks old* (for compilation for this work). '*Who can even keep documents looking this good*'? Certificates, report cards, court papers, pictures, vinyl record covers, etc. And in the midst, my siblings and I received the absolute best of old school parenting, which is highly incomparable to today's generation.

'*Downtown Pat Brown*,' is brassy and classy, strong as iron and tough as nails. She never drove but, would and *still can* beat you to a destination on two to three buses, '*with her roller buggy*,' chair in tow, even right now at a ripe '*young*' age of 80! Back in the day, she would walk

5

everywhere also! We'd often be traveling right behind her. Our trots reminded me of the big duck and her chick-a-dee's that causes a car to stop, when you're traveling on the highway, to let them cross the road. *"Here comes Pat and all 'dem 'chil'ren!"* We often heard family members shout out as *"Mama"* would be leading us up the road to visit with other relatives, at their homes. And what a tease that was... along with laughs galore. Always a hard worker, rather it was *at the Watch factory, the Bars or University of Buffalo college*, (where she later retired from at the age of 58), her children would want for nothing. We may not have liked the *'brand'* of clothes or the choicest of *'meals,'* but we still *SURVIVED* and with *flying colors*; we were able to use what she gives to the reader in *"Pay Attention,"* to soar high; to overcome the challenges of everyday realities. *Which has been the best gift by far.*

Our Mother constantly put before us, not only, the ability to be independent, and resourceful, but shielded us from, *as much as she could*, the *ills* of the world; *while at the same time*, instilled in us how to love and respect other people.

Humbly Submitted,

Bernadine C. Taylor, Daughter

TABLE OF CONTENTS

I was born at Sisters of Charity Hospital, in Buffalo, New York on June 12, 1939. My family lived at 329 Jefferson Avenue, at that time. (The house still stands today... just a newer built model). There weren't *any* telephones during that era, *but* I was still so '*fast*' growing up. It didn't even make any sense as to '*why*.' I guess it was just the signs of the times with me, my Aunts, about five to six of my best girlfriends and *Cousins*. (So, I naturally *would* be *the one, by the way,* to have *the most girls*) and I was as strict as I could have been raising them; knowing how '*grown*' *I thought I was* when I was just a kid myself.

Reared by my Maternal Grandmother, Lizzie Mae Speed, "*Mama Speed*," who was married to my Grandfather, *Ike Speed,* (whom we called "*Papa*"), I learned a lot. *How to cook, iron, sew, clean up the house, and wash clothes*, (that we would hang outside on a clothes line, with these wooden clothes pins in the summer to dry; and in the winter, we would have to switch the clothes drying to the attic). *Mama Speed* also taught me how to *do* dishes... *you name it*! My Grandparents migrated from *Calhoun Falls, South Carolina*, and bore eight children, (*Curtis, Catherine, Mae, Junior, Gladys, Florence, Donald and Marshall*). My Grandmother only had a third grade education, yet was able to teach my Grandfather how to read. He was bent on learning how,

8

because he wanted to join the '*Masons*,' and there were rules and regulations, you had to know… but you had to know how to read them too. After he learned how to read, (my *Aunt Gladys* recalls), he read better than anyone in the group and amongst his peers!

I even remember when one of my Uncle's was born, '*Marshall*.' It was amazing that some of the nieces and nephews, in the family, were actually older than our Aunts and Uncles or cousins who was very close in age, (*like days apart even*), like my only brother *Jody Boy* and my *Cousin Barbara*.

"*Papa*" was a hard Bethlehem Steel worker, who would bring home wages of about $50 dollars per week… that was *BIG* money back then. *I got it honest…*Papa Speed drank their charter oak liquor out of an empty *Vienna sausage can…* it didn't even have to be rinsed out after they ate the little sausages. And my *Dad* drank his beer out of the bottle, while *Cousin Anna* drank Genesee cream ale beer right out of the mayonnaise jar.

You could buy a lot back then... Eggs was only .20 cents a dozen and a cup of rice cost was a mere .15 cents. A scoop of sugar, *out of a barrel*, was only .10 cents, a loaf of bread only .03 cents. A Newspaper was .05 cents and we could ride the City bus for .03 cents *too* and I remember when it jumped up to .05 cents and so on and so forth. We had a '*Milk Man*,' but he would get paid on Friday's and "*Mama Speed's*" '*Bed Spread*' guy's tab ran her about $5 a week, (for the bedding that she bought *on credit*). Everybody had those blankets. They were called

9

'*Peacock*' spreads, because of the large peacock print that was dab smack in the middle.

We had to sleep on pallets, that we laid on the floor and once we woke up, in the morning, we would have to roll up the thin mattress pallets and put them in the closet. Rats would be running over our heads, scattering, everywhere. (*I guess they said it was time for them to get up too*). The rats were so bold, we would miss breakfast, sometimes, because of them. One morning, "*Mama Speed,*" was too scared to swoosh one rat away from sitting smack dab on top of the oatmeal box. There was no such thing as '*Borax,*' or other kinds of poisoning yet, so we would have to seal up the rat holes with empty plastic *Pepsi Cola* bottles.

I remember being only about 14 years old, when I would sneak into the bars with one of my Aunt's. I was like her little sister anyway. Her name was *Florence Speed.* I would dress up like a man to get into the Tavern and once inside I would have the *Patrons* buy me and my Aunt a beer! You could put .25 cents in the '*Juke Box*' and play FIVE records, (that's how I started loving "*The Blues,*" and enjoyed listening to all the greats…. "*B.B. King, Miles Davis, Muddy Waters, Coltrane and the likes*!" Jazz, Rhythm & Blues, Rock-n-Roll were favorites also.

When pay phones did arrive on the scene, it was only .25 cents, with unlimited calling too. *You could call anybody you wanted*! I was young, *but oh so excited*, to be present when my *Aunt Florence* spoke during the *Elk's Parade*. That was '*history*,' in the making, all by itself!

1

God Bless the Child…

My Parents were *Catherine Speed* and *Joseph Francis Brown*, and during the time that they were first married, it was just two children; me and my oldest Sister, *Gwendolyn*, who's two years older than myself. They separated for a while, but later my three other siblings came along. (*Burnett Catherine, Arlene Ophelia* and my baby brother *Joseph Sylvester Brown,* who we fondly call '*Jody Boy*,' til this day). Good, bad or indifferent, my Mother chose to name my baby sister's middle name after my *Father's* mother, *"Ophelia,"* and gave my knee sister, *Burnett,* her middle name, *Catherine* and my middle name *Elizabeth* after my Grandmother, "*Lizzie.*" We weren't allowed to ask a lot of questions about our parents' marital affairs, *not unless of course*, you didn't care about your bottom lip.

Looking back, it made perfect sense that I was shielded from '*some things*' but *boy-oh-boy* exposed to *way too much* of *everything else*. Children live what they '*see*.' Indiscretions was at an *all-time* high and *St. Mary's Catholic School* at the corner of *Broadway and Pine* Streets, did very little to keep me grounded, (although we had to daily quote *10 Hail Mary's full of grace*, the *Ten Commandments*, ten times, recite the *23rd Psalms* and '*The Lord's Prayer*' and had to even wear a white beaded rosary with a cross around our neck, (and pray with it *in a*

12

T-motion over our food, and for '*Lent*' services or when in dire straits).

I lived with "*Mama Speed*," at *544 William Street* and every journey was within '*walking distance*.' Once at Catholic School, I had to attend *Church first* then off to the classes. My Father's Cousin, *Jack* lived nearby at *William and Cedar* Streets; he was a ball of fun as a big Cousin, whose nickname was '*Baby Jack*,' even as a grown man, (he had a sister name Annie and his mother was also named Annie). There was a drug store on the side where his Mother, (*Mother Gaskin*) lived in the adjoining apartment building. I was very close to my big male Cousins, and their wives *Geraldine* and *Dorothy*, and my *Godfather, 'Big Apple*,' whose real name was *John Wesley Burch*, a very austere, yet humble man, and great in stature, (*And* also, one of the biggest '*Number Runner's*' in the Community), who also lived close by, at the corner of *Hickory and William* Streets, (in a red brick building).

I sent my youngest daughters over to my Godfather, *Big Apple's* house, because my hands *were full* and I was always at some '*Ball*,' *Card game* or a *Bingo hall* and I knew '*Big Apple*,' the '*GOOD Deacon*' down at the *DeLaine Waring African Methodist Episcopal (AME)* Church down on *Swan and Seneca* Streets would take my girls with him to Church. *And he did.* Seemed all our life was '*DOWNTOWN*.'

Luckily for me, he put them on the Choir and Usher Board for me too! But, when my daughters would

13

come back home, they would ask me a whole bunch of questions, they'd seen outside of the 'Church house' and would also tell me how they knew how to *play the numbers.* I jokingly told my *Godfather* when I arrived to pick them up, one day, that "*I left my daughters with you to be an example to them... to teach them something!*" He was so comical,

"*I did... you wanted me to take them to Church with me... I did and I taught them how to count money and how to drive a car!*" I laughed so hard. Not to mention, he made sure they went on all the YPT (Youth) Church trips; held in New York City. They were thrilled. Actually, he would babysit all my children for me. My oldest child was a little boy, but by the year of *1968*, the last of my *babies* (made nine) were already on the scene.

2

Babies having Babies

I bore my *oldest* son at *thirteen years old* on
Bennett Street off *Broadway*, in very close proximity to
"*Henry's*" our hamburger joint, (*way before the
McDonald's restaurant chain. Henry's Hamburgers
actually had a symbol of the big hamburger encircled on
it; with a man cheesing and sporting a white uniform with
a paper white cook's hat but when the 'golden arches'
came, it put "Henry's Hamburgers right out of business*).
It was my hang out spot *along with my wild girlfriends.*
We would *get money* from *their Uncles.* $5 and $10 was a
lot of money to us. And we knew which ones would give
the most. We'd buy a whole lot of penny candy, (tiny
brown paper bag *fulls)*, for a nickel and not only that…
loose cigarettes were only .5 or .10 cents. There was a
hotel building that sat on the corner of *Broadway and Oak
Streets.* We called it, the "*2 and 10*," because it was $2
dollars to '*get in*' and $10 to turn a '*trick.*'

I dropped out of *Catholic* school, around *nine
years old*, about *the 3ʳᵈ grade*, but had already knew
reading, writing and arithmetic and *did I mention*… an
excellent cursive writer by then, (although later I was able
to get back into school). It was a new Elementary school
called '*Fosdick-Masten*,' where the teachers still tried, as
best as they could, to keep the genders separated. There
were two entrance doors located on the *Best Street side* off
of *Masten Avenue*; one door for the '*Girls*,' and another

15

door for the '*Boys*,' engraved above, 'til this day, but it is now called *City Honors*. Later on, I attended School #12, where I learned how to "cook and sew." I never will forget I made my own skirt, a little ole' green skirt that I loved so much.

Fast forward, for a moment, July, year 2019, my youngest son tried to make reference to my level of education, by stating "*I didn't go beyond the3rd^h grade*," in conversation, during a visit, while I was hospitalized, no less… to my *not* understanding today's texting and Facebook technology, when speaking (*in front of me*), to one of my grand-daughters, (*I don't miss much*), but I'm 80 now, and just said to myself, '*but least I got money… matter of fact, I got ever'thing a po' Ninja need.* A word to the wise to always remember in life, "*God don't like ugly, yet He still take care of babies and fools.*"

Nevertheless, when I found out, that I was pregnant, I had to tell my Mother and prepare myself for the consequences. My Mother, '*Cat*' wasn't as sweet as '*Mama Speed*,' so I was gearing up to get a beating. I would hope that her and my Father would be too drunk and pay me '*no mind.*' Though you'd never *catch* my Mother drinking, (she always had a glass in her hand…*just-a-sipping* all the time). Ladies, *she taught me*, were to always be '*classy* and *discreet*.' You didn't drink out of the bottle, nor walk down the street smoking a cigarette.

Yet, this *wasn't* even my first pregnancy, (my first son, *Bernard,* died at three months old, due to a heart murmur), but now with a second pregnancy, as a teenager, I paid *dearly* for this lesson, when I had to spill my guts to the *Court System*, because my Mother had to drag me down to the *Welfare Building*, to report that there would be an increase in our family size. They wanted to know the "*where, when and how this could have happened. Didn't they know*! We didn't know we were being *molested*, let alone how to spell it. I had to tell every detail, (*where's my 'Rosary' now*). I thought I was going to be arrested *rather than the man* that did this to me, (who by all rights would have been jailed for '*rape*,' had I told on him; as he was more than '*twice*' my age). So, I *testified* for my family '*to eat.*' With a new addition coming into the home, my Mother could get more '*food stamps*,' and lucky for me, my *real boyfriend*, was not going to walk away scotch-free.

3

A Closed Mouth Don't Get Fed

"Raise your right hand, and place your left hand on this Bible... you swear to tell the truth and nothing but the truth... so help you God..."

I received a *"Subpoena"* in the mail from Children's Court. It was addressed to me at 258 E. Ferry Street. *Downtown* and *Cold Spring* communities has proven to be my safety net throughout my life. It was always something to do or somewhere you had to be, but on the flip side, it was always somewhere to eat and places to go to get a drink, a beer or even somebody's party to attend. *Restaurants and bars galore*! One on every corner, near 'bout. Nevertheless, after getting this mail, I can't say where I landed but can say wherever it was, I had *had* plenty of Vodka to deal with it.

"You are hereby summoned to appear before the Children's Paternity Court, located at 134 West Eagle Street, on May 18th, 1961 (5th Floor) at 2:00 o'clock in the afternoon as a witness of the County's Social Welfare Unit, Commissioner Burke."

"A pre-court interview has been arranged for paternity action in the office of Mr. Quinton Martin, Assistant County Attorney, Room 918 on the 9th Floor, 210 Pearl Street at 10:00 o'clock in the morning. Bring with you any witnesses who will testify in your behalf."

"Yours very truly,"

ERIE COUNTY DEPARTMENT OF SOCIAL
WELFARE

Commissioner

I had better be more careful, but there was no time for that now. Especially since my Mother would still have to look after me… and after my testimony… she probably wouldn't care to besides the fact that I had no idea that I would be asked to testify anyway. For more food stamps and $10.00 per week child support… *what kinda mess is that*? I have exposed myself for 'chump change.' I need my own house for sure now. But it would take three more babies before that was accomplished. And the Court Stenographer in this case, held back no punches, so I know you don't blame me for not going for child support EVER AGAIN after this.

CHILD: BABY BOY BROWN, Buffalo General,
December 31, 1952

Weight at birth: 5 lbs. 2 ½ oz.

          Patricia receiving welfare aid for self and child.
This is Mother's and Child's only income. Welfare
Department. hospital bill for confinement. Patricia is
unmarried.

First Met Boyfriend: On street while going to and from
school; Patricia then attending St. Mary's School on Pine
Street between William and Broadway; while Boyfriend
attending at School #35 on Elm St. near Clinton. Patricia
went home for lunch with Sister and would meet
Boyfriend at Sugar Bowl, a delicatessen at Clinton and
Michigan.

First Relation: Fall, 1951, when weather cool and before
snowfall at 206 William; at night, after dark, on a Saturday
before Easter while her Mother was shopping.

Second Relation: About a month after first time; first floor
parlor at 623 N. Division St.

Third Relation: In April, 1952, second floor bedroom at
131 Bennett St. in afternoon. (After March 1952 period.
This was last relation with Boyfriend before he went into
Air Force in April or May 1952).

First Medical: Pre-natal clinic at Buffalo General about July or August, 1952; went with her Mother. Dr. at Clinic said she was three month's pregnant.

Letter to and from Boyfriend about Pregnancy: After Boyfriend. left for military duty, Norfolk, VA, he wrote indicating he hope her expected baby would be a boy.

October 1952: (About Halloween), Boyfriend home 'on leave. Lives with Mother, 131 Bennett St. (Patricia showing pregnancy at this time). Boyfriend stayed overnight, in October of1952 and again when 'on leave' at Christmas, 1952. During this leave, Patricia told Boyfriend baby is expected in December, but he made no comment.

Birth of Baby, Dec. 31, 1952: Boyfriend went to hospital with Patricia and her mother at time of delivery. Boyfriend remained during labor.

Other visits to hospital during confinement: Boyfriend sent $5 through mail before birth while he was in military service; he said it was forwarded so she could get a few things she needed.

WITNESSES:

PATRICIA'S MOTHER, 33 Edna Pl. saw him call on
Patricia and knew he slept with her in October and
December, 1952

PATRICIA'S OLDEST SISTER, 401 Madison Ave., lived
at home in 1951 and 1952 and saw Boyfriend when he
called and knew he remained overnight in October and
December 1952.

Patricia has no knowledge of whereabouts of her
girlfriend's sisters with home she and Boyfriend
associated.

But as I say, *"Every woman knows "who" the
Father of her child is…" regardless of what sperm donor
they blame. You see, we didn't have Maury, Steve, and
Judge shows, WE KNEW. Even if you do take it to your
grave with you. Believe dat baby!"*

4

They Wanna Keep You Barefoot and Pregnant

I tried to slow down *around about* the age of seventeen or eighteen. But prior to that, after school, you can bet your bottom dollar, I would be at the *'Sugar Bowl,'* that was past Clinton Street on Michigan Avenue. That was where me and my girlfriends went for ice cream, and to meet *'Boyfriends.'* A milkshake was a quarter! We also hung out at the *'Clover Leaf,* and *Club Savoy* and at that time, I stayed with my *God-Sister, Rose,* upstairs at 434 Michigan Avenue over the *'Michigan Avenue Hotel,'* (which was in close proximity to the "*HOTEL LAFAYETTE,*" where my younger Sister, born after me, Burnett who we nicknamed, Bon Bon, worked. Their sheets even had their name on it, that she would bring home to us). Anyway, that's how I learned how to *'tend'* bar and started serving tables. We would put the kids to bed and go out... yep... *right downstairs*! Those were "*GOOD TIMES.*"

So, after a while, you take on jobs that teenagers usually take on; that of course, being "*BABYSITTING*!" Well, in the movies, girls get to put the toddlers and adolescents to bed, but during the late '50's, those doggone "*Father's*" of the children would put the *'Babysitters'* to bed. Thus, my two oldest girls were born from this most prominent *photographer* in all the "*LAND.*" (*Yes... the man, with the Magic Hand, a Black Indian from the Big Foot Tribe. They had rich dark skinned; longevity of life (his Mother lived to be over 90 years old, a very sweet woman with real nice wavy hair)*, glad to say, she loved her 'some me.' He tipped out a lot, but I loved his children, they called me, 'Mama too, *OR* 'Auntie.' You just didn't know what role to play. But the boys were great... mannerable and respectable, *til this day*.

I must admit, I was intrigued with the process of film... during this era, you would have to soak the parched paper in the tub to get the photograph, and then hang them up in the attic to dry out; to get your black and white copy. There weren't any colored photographs back then, just black and white. We didn't know what to do when the polaroid cameras came out, where you'd have to peel the back silky film off to display the picture. I still have one of those black and white pictures that I have of my *oldest two daughters Father* with *his other* two daughters on it, along with my oldest daughter, Cynthia, (*who was only six years old in the picture*). I noticed on the back of the thick white and black paper, many years later, that it had his '*signature stamp*' on it along with the telephone number: *TL4-2706, July 21, 1963*, along with the address. His Mother lived directly across the street, from my Father, (Joe Brown's) '*Cousin Manny,*' (*Cousin Anna's Brother*), in a house painted pink with green trim, and flowerpots aligned around the double (upper and lower) porch railing. One of the best houses on the block. A huge pink house; a double. And they painted it every year. And *boy, oh boy*, could they make some good homemade wine, out of grapes and put them into these big barrels. 173 Sycamore Street is where I lived then... (next to where Unity Baptist Church sits today).

At this time, had separated from his wife, which is why I really started *babysitting*. Our relationship didn't last too long, I ended up meeting another fella' (*for whom my third daughter was born*).

5

A Bitter Pill To Swallow

I loved my two daughters, Cynthia and Vanessa, and thank goodness for family all around me, to help me raise them. Even though, their Father and I didn't work out, they knew who he was. Still quite young, I was close with my mother's side of the family *and* my father's side, and I chose relatives on my father's side to help me raise my second daughter, (straight from the hospital). But, little did I know, they would change her name, and move her out to the *countryside.* I, at least, wanted access to my daughter, but they "*took her all the way*" out of my life. (My Father's cousins... his people... who were supposed to be '*my people*').

I remember when I went over to Cousin Marie's house, this one day, after taking all of my children with me, because Cousin Marie had given me a heads up that *my daughter* would be coming to visit. (*This was some years later, after ALL my children were born and of some size, my youngest son, was in kindergarten and my youngest daughter was around ten*). Cousin Marie was already helping me raise my 4th oldest daughter (*Scooter*). Her father. '*Sly*,' always said she was scooting out the way for the next one, *as if he didn't already have two sets of 'scooting' babies.* But, nevertheless, I had nine children in total, (the ones I kept, anyway, less the ones I lost... not to mention my last child, had a twin, but it fell in the toilet);

but all by age of twenty-six, and was known around my family and aunts of having '*the most.*'

After, the *tip off*, I packed up my children and said, "*We're going over to 'Cousin Marie's' house.*" They complained, asking '*why… what for… and do they all have to go?*' I said, "*Yes, you need to see Scooter, and there's someone else I want you all to meet.*" They didn't have a choice, of course, because at the end of the day, "*I'm Mama,*" *and what I say… goes!*" I had told them some years earlier, that they had another sister, that they never met, they just didn't know they were going to meet her this day. All along, for years, her and Scooter, would play together '*as Cousins.*'

I never drove, nor ever had my driver's license, so we walked… me and my tribe, following behind me (like little chickies following the Mother Hen) and before long, we were at *403 Monroe Street, off Broadway.* I only lived off Jefferson Avenue, in the Talbert Mall, 485 Clinton Street, a.k.a. "THE PROJECTS!" (*Ironically directly across from my mistress' building of 515 Clinton Avenue*), which I'll touch on later, (*maybe*).

Cousin Marie (and *Uncle TJ*) was so happy to see me and all my children, and warmly invited us in. We talked and laughed, and my kids met their other cousins, *Butch and Peanut* too. I started drinking heavily, and while we sent the children next door to the Community Center, called "*The Westminister,*" I couldn't wait to see 'MY DAUGHTER.' She arrived at the same time all the children were coming back from a youth program at the community center. They came into the house, with glee,

27

telling me excitedly about the program, and how there was even a spaghetti dinner. I nodded and said, '*good*,' as I urged everybody to sit down and yelled at them, to be quiet... to hear *what I gotta say*! They scrambled, knocking each other halfway down, some landed on the carpet, some ran in the living room on the couch, frightened.... And I just couldn't hold the '*pain*' in any longer, coupled with the '*serum truth*.'

"*You see, this girl right here, y'all been playing with all day...* (I pointed to my third oldest child), *she is NOT your Cousin... she is your SISTER!*" I was in the middle of the floor... no one moved... I started pulling my pants down, and allowed my stomach to plop out, to show the long diagonal curved scar that reached from the top of my stomach to the bottom. A thick, zipper line, and continued.... "*This is where she came from.... They had to cut me wide open to get her out... I like-ena-died.*"

"*Pat.. Pat... enough...that's enough*," Cousin Marie stammered over to me angrily, when she heard my daughter yell out with fear, "*WHO IS THIS WOMAN?*"

"*I AM YOUR MOTHER... they took you from me!*"

Cousin Marie, rushed to grab me, to sit me down. But it was too late... ALL of the children were crying, and rushed over to hug, their newfound 'Sister.' She only knew her one Sister, born after her, because *Scooter*, actually lived with Cousin Marie. I was young, and had just had too many children, to care for all at once. My youngest baby girl, lived with another Cousin... needless

28

to say, this daughter was the only one, who when sent to live with relatives, was actually taken from me. I regret it, but "*you can't cry over spilled milk.*"

It would be a little over a decade before we would cross paths again. Thanks to Scooter, my 4th oldest daughter, who continued to keep in touch with her big sister over the years, and would often attend her singing engagements. Her voice was melodic just like "Natalie Cole." Scooter also was instrumental in bringing Vanessa to see me. She gave me a picture of herself, and I put it on display right from my China Cabinet. I swallowed the pill, it was bitter… thank God for allowing me to last all these years to come to grips with it and to see all of my children into adulthood.

6

There's More Fishes In The Sea

Wilt, (my 4th child's *'real'* Father), was very jealous. He told Sly that it was a man in my house... lying on me, this one time, because he was now the *"Ex."* So, they got to fighting. Needless to say, I didn't stay with Wilt long, because he wanted to fight ALL THE TIME. He would have killed me! (Three different Dads in... were each twenty years my senior, so they knew *what they were doing*). Anyway, I would have to take him 'Downtown', all the time, as well...to report him to the Authorities so much, (*too much*). THEY KNEW MY NAME, for crying out loud. He was a *'low down dirty dog.'* It could have stemmed from his days in the *Military*, though, (he served in World War II). Back then, weren't no programs for *"PTSD"* for the Veterans, like today. They say, he had got wounded once, and had to get a *'metal plate'* put in his head, which had to be true because, he was *every bit of crazy.*

One time, I had to hide under the bed and in the closet at my Cousin Anna's house, but he even slapped her, when she wouldn't give up my location and would even wait it out; him and Uncle Joe would drink so long, (while he waited for me to come out of hiding), but would soon burn out and would eventually leave. Once he left, I would run down the street, go pick up my oldest two babies, grab his baby from Cousin Anna's house and head to Aunt Helen's. Lo, and behold, he came there... but

Aunt Helen was nothing to play with. He came to her house one time, and she said, "*UNT-UN, THAT'S THE LAST TIME, you gon' hit her... get on away from here and let the door knob hit you where the dog shudda bit'cha!*"

And that was the '*straw that broke the camel's back.*' My third daughter, who we nicknamed, "*Colt 45,*" was born on February 25, 1959 at 347 William Street, (looked just like him, with long beautiful hair... he was of Indian descent... as we all are, but you could really tell and she looked like me as well though), needless to say, that relationship was over.

Cousin Anna took a lot of *licks* for me, that term wasn't referring to drugs back then, but actual hits from my abusive children's father's. All of them were abusive, and I didn't have sense enough to leave them alone, right away, *that is*. But, eventually, I did, but not without one or more of their babies.

As my daughter got older, she asked, '*why don't I marry her Father... for his money?*' I told her, '*I don't want it.*' He was too abusive!

Decades later, he ended up marrying my '*Ex Sister-in-law*' and she had two sons for him, (she was told by the doctors that she couldn't conceive... neither did she have any with my Brother, but she was very dear to me and *helped to raise my children when they were babies.* She was also the step daughter of Cousin Anna's brother, *Cousin Manny*); but she would call me over to their house when he would beat her (and hers were pretty bad beatings too) and I would have to go over there (to her rescue) and

31

talk some '*sense*' into him or even spend the night with her to ward off his attacks, (strange as that would sound).

But that just how it was. *There was no way, I was going to allow that*! Even when she would threaten that she was going to call me... he would stop most times. *Hell, I was crazy too* and he knew I wasn't scared of him... I just knew, *I wasn't ready to die*; it was better to be "*safe than sorry*," in my book. Eventually, he stopped. It took a while, but he gradually calmed down, could have been '*old age*.'

7

Back in the Day

My Aunt Helen, was an awesome woman; she was
my Paternal Grandmother's *Sister*. A great woman, she
taught me how to cook. Spaghetti was our favorite! We
would chop up onions, green peppers and celery. She
would tell me that adding that celery to the sauce *gives it
such a special flavor*. I was happy to have my great aunts
and cousins and grandmother around, because BACK IN
THE DAY, they taught us so much, as I said earlier, we
knew how to sew, wash clothes, keep a clean house and
wear clean underwear every day… some things *have to* be
passed down.

It's funny when you think about it, but it was
forbidden to wear underwear with holes in them, because
as my ancestors put it… if you were ever in a car accident,
no one wants to see that; we were told it was
embarrassing, even the boys too. Every time you stepped
out of your house, BACK IN THE DAY, you had to have
yourself TOGETHER!

And you dared not go out anywhere if your house
wasn't clean. We ironed, we sewed, we were clean! We
had to wear stockings, and no flip flops or flat shoes nor
did we wear shoes without no socks! By golly, we
couldn't even wear shoes with our '*toes*' out. We couldn't
get our ears pierced, so I would sneak and wear "*clip
on's*."

The man had to walk on the outside of his wife or girlfriend, blocking her from the street and it was tacky for a 'Lady' to walk down the street smoking a cigarette and disrespectful for a man to spit on the sidewalk, while a lady was walking by.

My Great Aunt Helen, bought a house, BACK IN THE DAY, where we spent a lot of family times together. *Uncle Louie* was *Aunt Helen's brother* and *Aunt Helen Anderson* and *Aunt Helen Cotton were Sister-in-laws*.

"74 DUPONT" was where so many of our family gatherings and holidays were held. It was a very good house, including an in-law apartment upstairs. No one but family lived there. (Aunt Helen and my Father's Mother, Ophelia were sisters, by the way). When Aunt Helen passed, she *willed* the house to our "*Cousin Anna,*" (my Father's Cousin), and when she passed, God rest her sweet *sweet* soul, she *willed* 74 Dupont to me.

Cousin, Big Dee, who lived in Rochester, would often take us driving in his camper. (I took care of his son, Tykie, when we lived at 30 Milnor Street); Aunt Helen had a big house with a backyard just as big with hammocks on the tree. I remember this from when I was just nine years old. Nevertheless, Big Dee, would go over to Canada to buy Canadian bacon... paid good money for his meat too. His 3rd wife was a beautiful spirited woman named "*Vee*" and she was an awesome Foster mother of *Dwight, Demond,* and *Theresa.* Big Dee was my Father's Cousin and I was privileged to be close to both my Mother and my Father's side of the family, growing up as were my

34

children, (*The Cooks, The Gaskins, and Gaffey*). And there was also *Cousin Juanita* (my Cousin and my Friend) and her husband, *Murphy* and their children, *Monie, Michael, (Mad dog) and Raz...* I mean, just a bunch of us. We were all close like nobody's business. *And we partied*! That's another reason why, I'm called, "*Downtown Pat Brown*," you couldn't out dance me either... Ask one of my granddaughters, how we *cut da rug* at her 21st birthday party.

We never did go hungry... *Nobody did...* back in the day! Everybody had food! And even when the electric was off, I would sit the milk out on the windowsill in the winter to keep it cold or cook meals on a hot plate.

215 Cedar Street was where we would go and *Cousin Sidney* she would feed you too; *lima beans* and *hot bisquits*, pat them bad boys and throw them in the oven... right out of flour and lard, water, buttermilk! There wasn't no '*bisquick*' back in those days... no criscoe and shit, you'd betta get you a bucket of lard and save the grease. We would boil a slab of salt pork and then fry it; that was our meat. And one Meat Market had to close down because it was selling, '*horse meat.*' We was buying it and hooking it up though... but then '*word*' got out that it wasn't beef at all!

Back in the day, *you know us*, we would make '*hog guts,*' taste like a delicacy. I still clean '*chitterlings*' for my children. I remember one time, I even took some to my daughter, at her Church, (knowing I was going there for a program). I told one of my other daughters, don't let

35

me forget that bag under the pew, and when she asked me what was in it, I said *"Ann's chit'lins."*

Also, there was the *Washington Street Market at Ellicott Street*, where we would have to go grocery shopping, after the war. (Near the Hotel Lafayette, where my Sister, Burnett, use to work as a Maid). The Washington Street Market was housed in a big building where we had to go inside and get meat and stuff, (much like attending a Fair). On Saturday, we had to get a paper bag or cart (that's why I still take my bags now, when my girls come take me to the store), and even though I never drove, (because I was too scared) I still could beat you going anywhere on two buses. It was just something about how the cars maneuvered and at night, the lights would just get too busy for me. I had learned at one time, but just never took to it.

But there again, "BACK IN THE DAY," we walked everywhere anyway.

Before cars!

8

Street Feet

It was so many bars to go to... we couldn't just stick to one. There was the *Jamboree, Pixie's, The Pine Grill, Lloyd's Lounge, The Shining Light, Anna;s Tavern, Arthur's Pub, Lee's Lounge* and *Leon's,*(which used to be on Fillmore and Woeppel right next door to Matties, (before he moved it to Bailey Avenue; that's where I also use to work). We was running everywhere... But, at "*416*" you would see *any and everybody*! That's where *Mama* worked. Everybody knew her as '*Cat*.' It was on William Street, not far from *Aunt Emmaline* and *Uncle Ruffin's* house on *Howard Street*.

I would love hanging out with their daughter, my Cousin, *Joanne* and my friends, *Bernice* and *her sister*. We had a bunch of kids by this time, so I would babysit my friends children, while they went out, '*drankin*. Up above... over our house was a garage and the men would fry fish on the stove, but we had to use coals. They would get the wood, chop it up, throw some coals in there, and let the fire get hot and it would be '*on*.' We had to fry in '*lard*,' and we also had to make our own *butter*.

I remember on more than one occasion when Sly would be working the bar and thought he was going home with somebody else, "*Naw naw, buddy... you bringing yo' tail home tonight*." The nerve of him to dress me and his Mistress alike. *Some powder blue 'get-up*.' I was sitting

37

at one end of the bar and she at another. *She was going to find out how this works*, *"tonight!"* She had kids for him and so did I. And I bet your bottom dolla' I didn't hesitate to call on him when mine needed milk and pampers.

One of Sly's sons had drawed a knife on me... put it up to my throat and Sly got on him real good... (He must have figured out that I wasn't da doggone on babysitter, afterall). It was *cool runnings* though, because wherever you saw Sly, *you saw me*. He was the love of my life. Twenty years my senior (which is why I guess I couldn't be mad later on in life, at one of my daughters, who married a man, twenty years her senior), because your children *might* just relive some things you did; *good, bad, or indifferent*, so I tried to make it good.

My youngest Sister, Arlene, was the funniest, though... she would get so mad at me, because I would always ask her to watch my kids while I go out but when she would ask me; I would be so busy and never would watch hers. She covered for me on many occasions, but every now and then, she'd find a way to hang out with me. (I thought I was her Mother as well as my little and only brother, *Jody Boy!*)

Sometimes, I would be intoxicated and wet the bed, and when Sly would wake up, I would blame it on one of the children. (Since they would wet the bed so much, anyway til I had to buy an alarm mat to make them stop. It would buzz really loud, if you have an accident, and they would jump straight up and go to the bathroom). I think it was one of their bigger sisters who was against it, so I got rid of it, but I bet they got the picture.

But, this one time, I was so intoxicated, I made it all the way into the house, straight to the toilet and hugged the bowl, throwing up all over the place, but was so pooped, I ended up falling the sleep that way. When Sly came home, he thought that I never came home from going out, (*which happened quite frequently*), but not this night. He stormed out, going all over town looking for me; even down the street to my sister Arlene's house (who I affectionately call '*Sista*,' til this day. We'd even follow each other back and forth down the street, walking each other home at least 2-3 times a day. She lived at one end of Elm Street and I lived on the other); but nevertheless, when he finally came back home after exhausting himself, I was in bed. He said, "*Where were you?*" I said, "*In the bathroom… the whole time.*"

I'm still not sure if this was the same night, that he took his handcuffs, and hand cuffed my arms to the sides of the bed post or not. He was a Police Officer, (always thinking he was above the law because of it too). He worked at all the bars, hospitals and shopping stores.

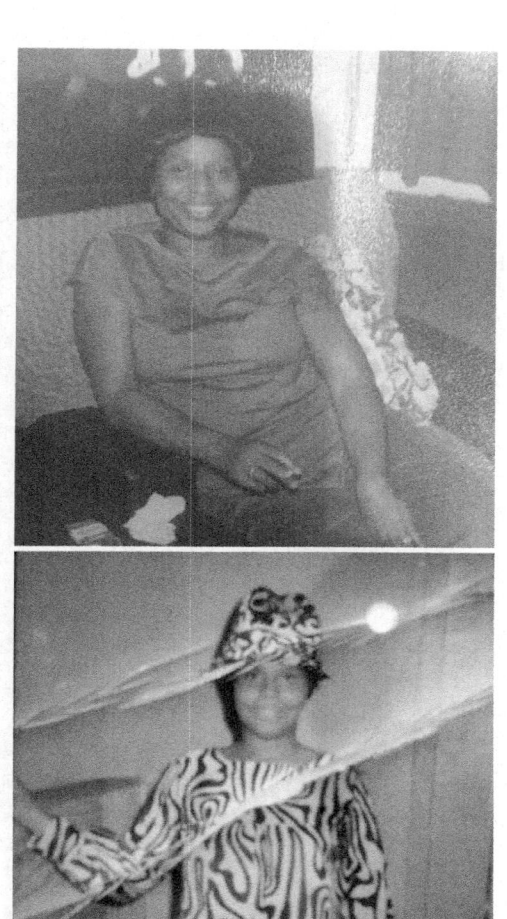

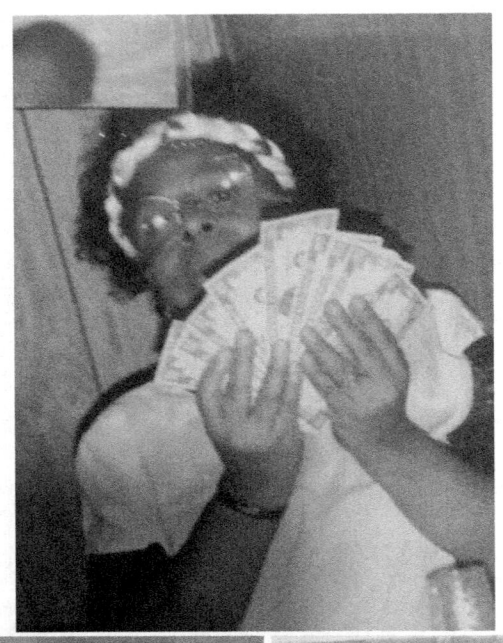

E & F Young's Grocery in the heart of Cold Springs.

Leon's Bar on Bailey

Chevy Ball Queen - 1962

This photo was taken from the March 30, 1962 photo files of the Buffalo Criterion Newspaper, and shows from left, Florence Speed, winner of the Chevy Ball Queen Contest. She was presented a crown and a trophy, $50.00, a 3 year membership in the NAACP, a certificate for three hair styles, a case of Libby's Club Beer, and $10.00 for "Miss Spring Dance".

Ms. Speed is shown here with her friend, Lentha Walters, at the VFW Hall at Hunt Shelter, March 30th.

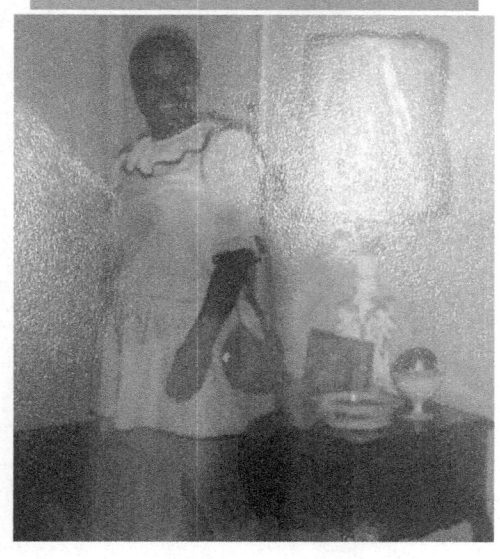

1965 Bardols Bar

Juneteenth late '70

2009

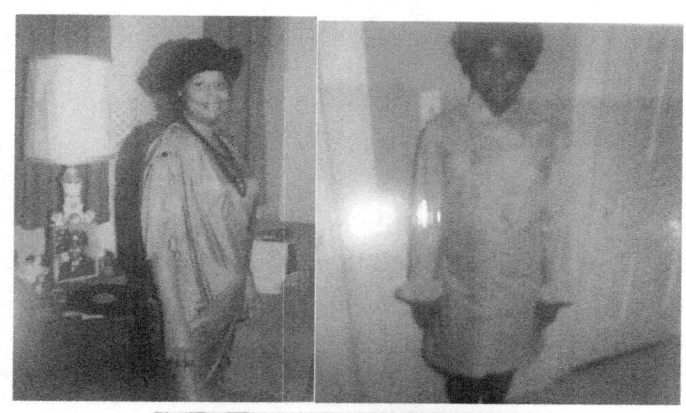

9

Can't Slick The Slicker

BINGO was an all-time favorite of mine; but so was Card and Game Clubs formed by me and a bunch of my girlfriends. I was going to card parties way before I got into a card club. We played bid wiz (the winners drink, the loser don't... for a $1... we called it DRINK OR SMELL).

Someone stole my wallet and once I found out what 'man' did it; (Blunt, the Number Runner), I went up to him, and put a gun up his one nostril, and told him, "*You gon' give me my money.*" And he did... *He gave me my money.... Hun! Messin' wit me... play wit fire... you gon' get burnt*! $80 was a lot of money back then! And I got '*mouths*' to feed! Humpf, he couldn't have thought. I fought my own battles, in the Streets.

We also played *Pokeno, Black Jack, Tunk, 500 Rummy, 3-Card Molly* and on a good night, *Poker*... Nowadays, I just play the *Slots*. I told my one grandaughter, (*I call her Mama... because one day she took me to the grocery store and gon' tell me I couldn't buy no ice cream... she can't go to the store with me no more*), but "*I been gambling all my life,*" when she told me, "*Grandma, you shouldn't blow all your money in the slots.*"

I heard myself tell her, "*Gurl, don't tell me... I used to blow the rent money back in the day just gambling!*

One time, I gambled all the rent money, and when the Landlord did come to collect, he felt so bad for me, because I had so many kids, he told me to just pay one month of the behind rent, and the other money use to buy my children's Christmas toys." I laughed so hard.

You would have thought I had won the *"Jackpot,"* at Bingo, *for which a lot of times I did.* I was living at *563 Elm Street* then, (moved there around '62 – '63), way before *Buffalo General Hospital*, had expanded. (By the way, I had all of my children at Sister's Hospital, if I didn't tell you that already… right where I was born). I guess that's just what people did, if you were *Catholic*, you went to a Catholic Hospital. (Sister's Hospital still stands today, same place, 2157 Main Street).

But, in 1968, my children cried when the duck pond was removed, in an effort to expand Buffalo General Hospital, and thus, the *"Fruit Belt"* would continue to suffer one 'Mulberry, Peach, Grape and Orange' Street at a time. My Aunt Florence's house served as family gatherings for many years… I never will forget that house… *144 Mulberry*!

My baby sister Arlene lived down the street from me with her husband and four children at *511 Elm Street* and my best friend, *Irene,* lived directly across the street from me (next to our delicatessen), which had got robbed this one day and we thought that the robbers were going to come after our houses next, since we lived so close. (My best friend, Irene and I had our babies on the same day that year too, March 3, 1968), and my 5th youngest daughter,

Ann, fell out of the upstairs bedroom window on Elm Street too, and somebody caught her. Thank goodness!

So much was going on during these years. But I never let nothing stop me... I would push a baby buggy with the hood with my three babies in it... and when the gas was off, I would have no problem cooking full course meals on a hot plate until I got the gas turned back on.

Dr. Martin Luther King, Jr. was assassinated, a month after I had given birth to my last child as well as both '*Kennedy's.*' Following that explosive year, nearly every home you visited had a large cloth material type frame hanging on their wall, with Dr. King in the middle, and President John F. Kennedy, assassinated in November of 1963 and his brother Robert Kennedy on the opposite side, who had been assassinated in June 1968.

It wasn't too much longer, that I moved to *137 Archie*, right across the street from *Cousin Anna*. The 1970's were proven to be much better, even with my children finding out that they had other brothers and sisters.

10

Save A Stool For Me

Revelot Bar.... was located where *Gigi's* Restaurant used to be... that's where I met and fell in love with *"Sly."* I was single, fast, and was on welfare. I would leave my three oldest children with my relatives when I would go out, only had three by this time (because remember, my fourth oldest child, I gave up to my Cousins to raise for me, right from the hospital, an unofficial adoption... you could say). Hardly ever, they changed her name and moved her out to the Country to be raised. I regretted it, resented them and wish I had been in a better position mentally, to keep her but my oldest son, I had already lost, and then my second son's entrance into the world, was *"Mama's baby, Daddy's Maybe,"* and then here comes the Photographer Dad of my next two; both girls. I really was the teenage *'babysitter.'* (What did I know?). So, you figure, by18 years old, at the most, I already had had four children, and mourning the loss of even one of those.

Sly got me an apartment that next day, at 238 East Ferry Street. He had talked to the Owner at the bar where he worked and wouldn't you know I *dun* laid down and had another baby, (*'gots'sta be more careful.'*). That was 1960, my 4th daughter, *Scooter*. She was born at 3 lbs., a 'premie' and had to stay in the hospital for a month. (Then, the following year, we moved to 260 East Ferry

Street and here comes another surprise bundle in 1961. *Two girls for Sly*!

He would give me money, so I could go and buy some Sunday dinner at Russell's (at the corner of Sycamore and Michigan Streets sometimes). *Hush money*! I would take money from him too and he didn't even know it. I would then play a number for *.50 cents to win $7*. Nobody was going to '*Ssh*' me... I had a big mouth... *and what came up... came out*! I use to 'roll'... I was turning 20, but Sly was whorish too!

One night, I went out... he thought I went to the house party; but I went to the bar on the corner of Riley and Wohlers Avenue, '*Polly, Jr.'s*' and here he come in there with *two other hoes*... telling me to go home... I wasn't going nowhere...

Me and my Sister ran the Jazz Bar! I was always out dancing... sometimes in the middle of the Street... jumping out of cars, at that! I could name every bar from Sycamore Street... *on down*. Then there was this bar named, "Costello's," that my Sister used to go to also... some of the most *Tip Top* niggas use to live it all up!

Barbados Bar used to be located at Broadway and Michigan Avenue. Sly was a Bartender and the Policeman, along with his best friend, "*Jimmy Hunter*," another Officer, and a good friend who remained throughout the years, (that's where I met Sly at... *at Barbados*).

Sly later worked at Sheehan "*Emergency*" Hospital, (way before ECMC came into play) and *Twin Fair* (*your modern day Walmart*).

Our local cleaners, was called, *Jimmy Ruffin's* right at Bennett and Broadway Streets; then later on relocated to William Street; where you'd find our local meat Market, *Kulick's* and also a little store called, *Funky Pauline's.*

I like to think of the song, "*Papa was a rolling stone*," by the Temptations, as Sly's '*theme*' song... "*wherever he laid his hat was his home...*" because every time, I wanted him, I called him. I would call his *wife* too and tell her, "*these babies need milk and diapers.*" I bet he came and brought me *that* money... '*Hell, I got babies too!*' I didn't care that he was mad, because he certainly was, (and would want to fight me too)... I wasn't scared of his *ass* either, standing damn near six feet tall, with twenty years between us; because I took care of *her* kids, when *she* was in the hospital... me and my baby brother *Jody Boy*. His third oldest son, tried to draw a knife on me, but that was his last time, trying to come for me... Sly set him straight.

My last four children were born back to back with her last four... and when I say... "*BACK-TO-BACK*," I mean "*BACK-TO-BACK*!" I could have him anytime I wanted. One *Mother's Day,* we were even dressed alike, because he bought us the same matching outfits. *He didn't care*; so neither did I... when I noticed our outfits. I strutted in *Woodlawn's Tavern* and sat at one end of the

Bar and she at the other end… *'we saw who was gon' out sit who… and it wasn't gon' be me!'*

11

Buy What You Want

And Beg For What You Need

I caught the '*Welfare Man,*' coming out of the house, one day. "*Mr. Nowicki*!" I couldn't stand that man! He used to make me mad. Back in the day, they would just show up at your house, (to be noisy)… *see what you got new*; just to make sure you still needed their '*Services.*' Half the time, you would have to hide shit all over the place, the iron, t.v.'s, appliances. *I would tell him what I wanted to tell him…* especially when he would question where *any one* of my children's *Father's were.* I told him, "*her Daddy got killed in a car wreck or for the other ones… they dead.*"

Then, I called their *Grandmother*, (Sly's Mother) and she would send a *telegram* to corroborate my story. *She lived in Washington, DC.* I even met Sly's one and only Sister, through *his Mother* and every time she would visit, we would hang out "alot," and go to all sorts of '*Balls.*" We would wear some bad gowns too!

Johnny's Ellicott Grill was *on and poppin'* too back then. It was located at *Ellicott* and *Genesee Streets.* Sly and I would "*ROLL*"…. '*Save that stool for me,*' I'd yell out. We drank all kind of Scotch… *Johnny Walker Red, J&B*, you name it. Sly's favorite choice of liquor was *Vodka*, mixed with orange juice and he smoked '*Parliament cigarette's*' (and always had one behind his ear). I smoked 'Salem's' for a long time... they were only *.50 cent a pack*! Nowadays, I have to get my *baby sister, my grandson,* (*Third*), or my 5th oldest daughter to take me to the '*Reservation,*' to get 'em now.

I later moved to the '*Projects,*' same thing was still occurring... hiding appliances. I couldn't wait to go to work. All of my children, my tribe, by now, was of age, and I didn't know how long I would be able to endure these 'Projects.' When the elevator was out of order, we would have to walk up five flights of stairs with groceries, no less. I was back, however, with my '*Road Dogs,*' (*Sis' n' nem*), but had to contend with the 'Gangs,' trying to recruit my children, like the *Mattadore's* and *Phythons*, and the girls, they named the *Phytholettes*. My heart was torn to pieces as I looked out of my fifth floor window, one evening, and saw a large gang of kids about to jump one of my daughters, for which she lost a front tooth from that ordeal. Good thing we knew large families, even Sly's sons came to my children's rescue. They knew who one another was now... oh well, they won't be the first... and sho'nuff won't be the last that have step brother and sisters.

One day, my baby son, '*Maine,*' came home, and said a woman threatened him on his way home from school... while she waited at the bus stop and said pointing her finger at him, "*SLY IS NOT YOUR FATHER.*" My son ran all the way home. I wanted to go to the building across the yard and whoop her tail... but I just told Sly... (by this time, we had long parted, it was around 1975); and I finally was getting some '*Child Support.*'

12

Can't Keep A Good Woman Down

I finally got to working, at a plastic bag factory first and so now, by this time, you wouldn't get *'home visits'* from *'The Welfare Department,'* they would just call you on your home phone; askin' all type of questions; threatening to cut my food stamps and cash assistance (but I wasn't gonna let them take away that *good ole' peanut butter and Government cheese*), but nevertheless, *'they gon' say they gonna do this and they're going to do that and how I owe them so much 'back money,'*… I told that *'Caseworker,' I don't owe y'all a damn thing… if anything… y'all owe me for staying on Welfare so long, raising my kids!*" And then I hung up on him.

Wouldn't you know, I started working another job at a *'Watch Factory,' DOWNTOWN*; 701 Seneca Street, *(right at Swan Street)*, on the assembly line… which didn't do me a bit of good, because I had had a hangover one Saturday morning and boxes went everywhere when I fell asleep on the assembly line.

The *'Supervisor'* who *turned Friend* said, *"PAT… LOOK… SHUT DOWN THE LINE!"*

I said back to her, *"LOOK WHAT YOU DID!"* Cracking up and it was like we were inseparable from that day on… *til this day*. I nicknamed her, *'Girlfrien'*! After that, she tried to still act like she was my 'Supervisor,' but I would give her that 'evil eye' look and say, "I will quit dis' mutha'*******!" She would go 'toe-to-toe'... "Dere you go... every time you get mad, you talking about quitting." But she knew that I didn't like *if somebody said something to me.*

I eventually left too, but not without, '*Girlfrien'*... I was the one who got her a job out at the *University of Buffalo* with me; and we both were able to retire, *with a Pension... How do you like those apples*?" (In the words of my Godfather, Big Apple, the one and only John W. Burch)!

I was still doing what I wanted at these jobs, over the years. So, after some years, the other '*Supervisor,*' *turned Friend* (hahaha... I don't meet a stranger), *gon' tell me that someone said they would be reporting me... and write me up, after some years.*

I said, *"I don't give a damn about my housekeeping work*!" They tried to act like I didn't clean up this big ole' Mansion house with the original oakwood staircase... gon' rub their finger alongside it... said '*it ain't clean.*'

So, the next day, I called in; I told them *I was sick... I ain't coming in.* Off and on, I would then have my '*Ole Man*' call in but they stopped the relatives from calling in for you (*across the Board*). It wasn't long after, when I went downtown and filed for my *Retirement.* They had a party for me... *that I didn't want* and gave me a

$100 bill.   I went to *65 Court Street, (Downtown Buffalo)* to sign for my *New York State* Retirement! I signed my papers, at 58 years old on August 30, 1997 and here I am 80! *"I'm ahead of the game..."*

13

Mirror… Mirror On The Wall…

Make 'Em Beg… Make 'Em Crawl

I met *Richard* up in dere… Yup, hanging out in *"Arthur's Pub,"* another *'broke dick dog,'* is what we would call the men who *'ain't got a pot piss in and no window to throw it out of.'* But, *"Arthur,"* who the bar was named for, was my good friend *Inez'* husband's establishment. We would jump out of the car and be dancing all in the street. (Nope, that is not new what these youngsters do today). Musicians would autograph their photos for us. I had one autographed from *James Peterson*, whose son followed right after his footsteps, named *Lucky Peterson.*

I was fast and we would be partying all the time. Our motto was, *"The eagle's fly on Friday, Saturday, I go out to play… Sunday, I go to Church and kneel down to pray!"*

"Arthur's Pub," would be booming back in the day. It sat on the corner of Genesee and Jefferson Streets, (he later moved his bar from there to the *"600 Club"* located at 600 East North Avenue). But getting back to this here *Richard* fella…. I ended up still bringing him home. I lived on *Chenango Street*, way on the *West Side*, by this time. That relationship was fun but fleeting. After all those years of living downtown and in what we called 'Cold Spring, here I am way 'cross town.'

Hegs, in *Cold Spring*, we even had our own Cab Services, "Cold Spring, Broadway and Fillmore," were the most popular ones. We owned our own 'Corner Stores.' We had Liberty Taxi and Yellow Cab drivers, also. They were around; but not like ours. From the grocery stores, we would hail what we called a "*Jitney.*" Our supermarkets were called *Bell's* and *Super Duper*. Tops wasn't even heard of yet. And the mid 90's, we finally had "*FIGMOS,*" which stood for "*Finally, I Got My Own Supermarket,*" on Jefferson Avenue.

Our shopping stores were *A.M. & A's*, *Woolworth's*, *Neisner's*, *Liberty* and *Thom McCann Shoes*, *Hen's & Kelly's*, *Twin Fair*, *Norban's*, then later came *Hills* and *K-Mart*. Very seldom did we venture out to the *Eastern Hills Mall* or the *Boulevard Mall, (We had the Main Place Mall). And as a matter of fact, I never set foot in a Mall until 2013)*. There was, of course, always a "*Goodwill,*" where you could find just about everything you needed for clothes and what-nots. We also had the five-n-dime store called *D&K*, (while the Dollar Tree was a long way 'away' in the making).

Once I relocated to the West Side, after those projects were infested with rodents, I encountered every little store possible along with some pizza places like *Ganci's* where I could buy my children, slices of pizza's that the Italian store sold in a square, '*cold*,' for .25 cents, (it was delicious) and then there was *LaNova's*, when it was just a little hole in the wall before they blew up. We also had the neighborhood cleaners, "*Rotundo's*" and a liquor store, called "*The White Horse.*" (Shame, that someone actually stole the 'white horse' a few years ago), but I came home so proud this one day, announcing to my children of all the adventurous places I found, including their schools, but they found the *'Boy's and Girl's Club* on their own, called *"The Butler Mitchell."*

They still didn't like the West Side... they had no idea where they were... let alone how to spell the Street. Can't say I blamed them... we all had to make new friends, (eventually, they warmed up to it). Everything seemed foreign to them, until they learned that if they kept walking up West Utica Street, they could cross over Main Street and be back onto East Utica Street. We were the second black family that moved to the three-story apartment building; everyone else were White or Hispanic; even one mixed couple and a mixed family... it was a melting pot, as they say or one waiting to explode; and a bit of a culture shock.

I was just happy that by this move, all my children were teenagers and my oldest daughter had joined the Army and I was also helping to raise my oldest three grandchildren, who I affectionately called, *"Duke, Stanka'* and *Bubba."*

"Cheese-n-crackers!"

"Sly?! How you get my number?"

There was only one man... and one man only, who said that. Here, we go! *"Mirror, Mirror on the wall, I'm about to make him beg... make him crawl."*

Thanks to my daughter Scooter, who had somehow got in touch with him, or he had ran into one of her best friends, and that's how the story began all over again. Scooter was now a teenager and had left Cousin Marie's house, and her Dad was going to let her live with him (at least until after she had 'Stanka,' her son). He now had four more children, who were bi-racial, which didn't matter, other than the fact that the world was still getting use to it. And now, its about 19 children in total (including the ones that were not his biologically), *still a high number*. It was a nice reunion, short-lived, still good times, just like the old times. We were drinking one day, and he let our son take his car for a spin around the block, and he barely made it back, crashing almost into the apartment building; that was hilarious... we were just happy no one was hurt.

Some years later, we lost Sly, in 1985, due to health complications. I'm not going to even write about that whole funeral ordeal and all that ensued after... that's for another book!

14

I Killed 5

"For thou hast had five husbands; and he whom thou now hast is not thy husband…"

John 4:18

I don't get to attend '*Catholic*' Church, like in the olden days. Mostly, I'll attend Catholic Church for '*Good Friday* and *Palm Sunday*, or *Ash Wednesday*… but I do go to Church… *with my girls.* All of them go to a different one… *but they go* and guess what… they'll swing by and take me too. And I love when my girls come and take me to Church and I love how they visit one another at their several churches. *So, I did pretty good.* Or shall I say, I did the best that I knew how… considering what I had to deal with… *with their 'Father's.'*

It's a wonder, I'm still here; 'cause I ain't never wrong nobody, because "*Right is right… and right don't WRONG NOBODY!*"

Move over, *Zack, Kevin, Tim, Wilt*, and *Sly*…. For… finally, "*Mr. Brown!*" I had been knew dis' old nigga… another one, twenty years older than me… as they all were… guess I just liked older men. Well, when I introduced this man to my grown children, they weren't enthused, whatsoever.

They knew me… *"If I liked 'cha… I liked 'cha… and if I stop liking you… then it was simple… you were out of the picture."* Well, Mr. Brown, already had my last name, so I introduced him as… *"my Husband."* My children laughed at me, saying things like, *"So, when did y'all get married? And how come we weren't invited… And where did you meet him?"*

I whipped out a piece of paper… an 8x10 tan *'Certificate,"* proving my love. *"Here it is right here… our marriage certificate."* It was *'self-made.'* Well the wording was already on the store bought certificate; all I had to do… was have one of my daughters fill in our names… and *wah-la*… it was official… in my book. They laughed so hard! *"Okay, Ma… we're just going to see how long this last."*

My children, again, were all grown and gone by this time… and I had a ton of grandchildren, most of whom, I don't know because I wasn't your average *'Granny,'* so, unless my children came over with them… I didn't see them as much as I probably could have. But they know who I am ("Grandma Pat") and that's all that matters. I didn't like how they would add my name onto the 'Grandma,' part but after they told me why I understood, (it was because I wasn't my great grandchildren's ONLY Grandmother, and that is how they were able to differentiate). Now, that we've ALL gotten older, I think we've bonded more, but not when they were little and as fas as the great grandchildren, you can forget it! I only know, "Chocolate Doll." That's Stanka's sister, "Poopie's" daughter." I know her oldest daughter too,

72

"but her baby sister, is who I had the pleasure of nicknaming, as soon as I held her, I hollered, "*Dats Chocolate Doll!*"

Hegs, when my oldest son was sick, in 2010, and about to pass away, and all my grands were up at the hospital, I didn't know '*who was who*' then. I thought one of my granddaughter's girlfriends was a part of my tribe, and greeted her, ever so kindly, held her hand and said, "*I'm sorry, I don't know y'all.*"

My daughter said, "*It's okay, Ma, you don't have to apologize for not knowing all of your great grandchildren... this one is actually not yours, she brought people up to the hospital for us.*"

So, anyways, meeting Mr. Brown, really didn't phase them... they were all a lot like me... "*As long as I was happy... they were happy.*"

And that happiness was only strengthened in all of our lives when I would summons them to my house for parties, whether they were held in the backyard or in the house or at a club somewhere; so, we all got along with *Mr. Brown.* He was laid back... easy going... had as with some of the other suitors... finished sowing his '*wild oats*,' that made for a perfect union, *like a match made in heaven.*

Mr. Brown, probably thought I was playing with him; but I was serious about our relationship. *I wasn't 'nuttin' to play with, baby*! We had some fun times, even as I aged gracefully, headed towards mid-50's and he was already in his 70's… but I had to make mention of him and tie it in with the Lord, because… and I cross my heart, just like when I was a little girl, going to Catholic School; I am blessed to have survived, and still maintain my integrity, stamina, dignity and worth.

You see, all of the men that played an important role in my life, are all *dead and gone*, and I am left to tell about it. So, when I run into *old-timers*, and people that I know, in general, and they ask me, "*How 'um doin'?*"

My answer, and I chuckle when I say it, "*I'm good… I killed 5!*

To have outlived what I had endured, is truly a blessing. God has been good to me.

15

Call Girl

I was determined, as I usually am, to go to the Casino, one Sunday. *Baby Girl*, was supposed to take me, but she forget she had a mini Church convention and had traveled back and forth to Niagara Falls, NY, all weekend, so couldn't take me now.... *And I was going for her.* You see if you gamble enough, then you can get free rooms, free gifts, free play and this particular weekend, they were giving out cell phone holders for your car and I wanted to get it for her. I had already gotten my other daughter one. My youngest two daughters, always took me to the Casino, because they know how much I like to go, so they would oblige me every so often. And especially on my birthday! I wouldn't depend or wait on them, all the time though, because, I just take off and go myself. I never drove, but I will beat anybody to get to where I have to go... on the bus. Not just one bus, but sometimes, two or three transfer buses. *"You can't keep a good woman down."*

Lo' and behold, at 80, I'm still getting around... I don't let no green grass grow up under my feet! *Humpf*, I couldn't be still, this day, I got my push buggy, so if I get tired, while waiting for the bus or walking, I can sit and catch my breath. Well, I was sitting down, on the seat of my walker buggy and when I noticed the #18 Jefferson bus approaching, I stood up. But, apparently not fast enough, because the bus driver zoomed right on pass me. I'm sure he didn't see me. Years ago, the bus drivers would at least slow up, just in case anyone at the side... near the corner... running to the corner... would stop... but *not today*.

Nevertheless, I heard someone yell out, "*GRANDMA... GRANDMA!!*" I would have never thought, I would be called out... *because I never stood on a 'corner,' baby!* So, I looked around to see this car... just so happened to be the same car that I spotted a few minutes ago... calling me out. I had already noticed the queen size mattress on the top of the car's roof. I didn't think anything of it... I just said to myself, '*hmm, somebody moving.*' Well, to make a long story short, it was my grandson, "*Third.*"

He pulled over and said, "*Grandma... where you going?*" I said, "*Boi, I'm trying to get to the Casino.* So, he says, "*Hop in... I'll take you... but I just have to drop off my mattress at my new house.*" Of course, I agreed, since the doggone bus passed me up and I would get to see his new house also. Can you believe he drove from his old house, did a stint on the expressway, and then down Jefferson Street, without the mattress slipping, sliding or falling off... HE IS MY GRANDSON! He said, "*WHERE THERE'S A WILL, THERE'S A WAY!*"

We dropped his mattress off and went our way. I didn't have a lot of money that day to play the slots with, and my grandson, said he didn't have any money either, when I pressed him, so I acted as if I was ready to go, but I really wasn't... in my mind, I'm thinking, "*C'mon, for real, you don't have nothing.*" He' so very mannerable though; he even took me to the store so I can buy me a carton of cigarettes from the Reservation, while in the *Falls*…

But picking me up, on the corner, is how I got the title for this chapter, in my book, "*CALL GIRL.*" I laughed so hard because, in all my days, I have never been picked up on NO corner, "*if you know what I mean.*"

16

My Long Lost Friend

I was grateful for my daughter, Ann, who every Monday, would take me to the Casino, so I can play my "Senior Free Play" money. I had been frequenting the downtown casino ever since it was built in downtown Buffalo, right on Michigan Avenue right past Seneca St. (my old stomping ground). Whenever my daughter or my son-in-law took me, it saved me from having to catch two to three buses to get downtown or pay tons of money in cab fare. Most times, she would wait for me; knowing that that probably wasn't going to be my only stop when leaving the Casino. It was either going to be the Bank, Dollar General or the Dollar Tree.

This one day, in particular, I mumbled, *"Sure would be nice to go and see my good friend, who is at High Pointe,"* (which was a Nursing Home and Rehab Facility right near Buffalo General Hospital but on the Michigan Avenue side). Actually, a block from my old grammar school, Fosdick-Masten, but renamed City Honors.' I had mentioned it to my baby daughter, but I know how she couldn't take hospitals, all like that.

But anyhow, my daughter obliged me, this day, and we arrived at High Pointe facility, which was a spin-off from the old Deaconess Hospital, to see my old friend, her nickname was "B." I had seen her son, a few weeks back, and he told me that his Mother was in the Nursing home. I longed to see my friend. So, at the front desk, I couldn't remember her full name.

I was grasping, "*It's Beatrice, I think…. Um… um… Lofton.*" But, the guy at the front desk, couldn't find that name. So, he asked me, "*Could it be Lawton?*"

"*Yes, yes… I think so.*"

So, he gave my daughter and I, a pass to room #308. And lo, and behold, when we went to her room, there she was sleeping. I whispered, "B…B," to wake her. She focused on my face, and kept looking, then said, "Oh, Pat!! You found me." She teared up and so did I.

"*B*" and I go way way back; I was living on Elm Street. I used to date her Cousin, the "*Spaghetti Man*," we called him; who lived behind my baby Sister, Arlene house, on Michigan Avenue too. We had some good times. By then, I was in my late mid 20's and now the Lord has blessed me to see 80 years old, and I'm still visiting my friends at the hospital. My friend told me she couldn't walk anymore, but she was definitely a real *trooper*, because she always had one arm, for as long as I knew her, it's quite thin now. She put it under the sheet when my daughter was looking at it. But let me tell you, she would and could do everything…. Cook, clean, you name it!! And could throw back some booze.

Her husband actually used to call himself, liking *my Mother*, truth be told… but I stayed at their house a lot, and nothing ever came of that.

79

I was so happy to have been able to visit my long lost friend.

I moved into my new senior building almost five months ago, it was just a like convalescent home, so many residents had walkers, canes and oxygen tanks and if you stay in *High Pointe* too long, they would give your apartment away.

From there, my daughter, also had much patience with me and allowed me to check on one of my neighbors, who was also at High Pointe, for over a month now. The clerk gave us room #168 for her, and she was happy to see me as well. You have to check on your neighbors and friends because you never know…

EPILOGUE

If I die today or tomorrow...

I have done it all... I lived...

It's so much that I could have said, as you can probably tell... but I wanted to really relish about my *City*...and how I rolled in it! Talk about the Landmarks, the restaurants, the taverns, even down to the Cleaners... Like, "*Pendricks*!" (A fixture that was on the corner of Jefferson Avenue and Northampton Street). Tell of my upbringing, in the heart of *Downtown Buffalo, the Fruit Belt, Cold Spring, and the West Side*! And I wanted to reminisce about all of my *old stopping grounds* and get some things off my chest too.

At the time of my writing my Memoir, I have seen so much in my life's span, and I can truly say, I am happy to have been blessed to see so much. I still get around, and can't believe I now live in the same area where I raised my babies at. I remember, "*Gigi's, Dexter's, Jim Bell Cleaners*" and who can forget my people at "*Doris Records*," which is a landmark all of its own. (We miss you Luchey)! Speaking of records, I got 'em, baby... 45's albums, tapes, cd's of everybody, my greats! You name it... I got it! I use to sell them back to "*Record Theatre*," another landmark. But now I give them away. Even my *Rick James*' records... I went to his funeral!!

So much has changed. I wish I could find an old telephone book that had all of these places listed. Buffalo use to be thriving… *and it still is…* don't get me wrong… just in a different way… but we lived back then. I'm not called the dancing lady for nothing… we use to *boogie-woogie*! I recall the huge Mason parades going through William Street. Our movie theatres, *"Loew's Tech and the Apollo."* Good eating at *Swiss Chalet… Ponderosa…* and the *Crackle Barrel*, (way before the one on Transit Road). I really love the "Pine Grill Reunion!"

I enjoy going to the Casino and would go every day if I had the money, as I tell my family, *"that's my enjoyment."* That along with going to the "Broadway Market." Nowadays, I play my numbers at *"Mandella's"* and get my printing done at *"The Ink Spot."* On *Jefferson Avenue* still holding it down. I remember when *"Juneteenth,"* used to be held on Jefferson Avenue. *Do you*? Buffalo's rich history is alright with me… And if you go a little further up the road, (Main and Michigan) the building is still there where *"Freddie's Donuts,"* use to be. Even bowling alleys were a huge treat for me. I don't get out to bowl like I used to… but I still have my bowling ball (in a bag) and my shoes (I think my shoes have dry rotted a bit now), but when my oldest daughter, was living… she would take me bowling with her. I was on a whole league too, with her! She will be gone, five years now, come February 15, 2020… I miss her… time flies, and ten years for my oldest son, as of 2019… *but I'm still kicking for them.* I have my good days and on the bad days, for the little aches and pains, I say, *"OOOH, OUCH AND WOW"* and keep getting up! So, I say to all my family, friends…*"Keep Getting' Up & Watch Yourself*!"

PAY ATTENTION

Downtown Pat Brown's

Glossary *of her* Familiar Phrases

No News is Good News
Feed 'em with a long-handed spoon
You barking up the wrong tree
Let the door knob hit you… where the dog should have bit
you
You get dumber and dumber
Something gotta give
What goes up… must come down
The straw that broke the camel's back
It takes one to know one
Straighten Up and Fly Right
My mind don't fool me
No bet to me
Why buy the Cow… When you can get the Milk For Free?
The rich get richer and the poor get poorer
What one won't do… the other one will
A little birdy gon' tell it
You don't miss the water til your well run dry
You can't miss what you never had
Don't let the green grass fool ya
The grass always looks greener on the other side
Two wrongs don't make a right
You going out the world backwards
What goes on in this house…. Stays in this house
Don't take no wooden nickels

Where there is a will there is a way
What goes around comes around
It gotta get betta' cuz it can't get no worse
Can't kill nothin' and won't nothin' die
Manners will take you where money can't
Don't let your right hand know what the left hand is doing
He'll put no mo' on you than you can bear
If it was a snake… it woulda' bit cha'
Where's the beef?
One monkey don't stop no show!
Time don't wait for nobody
Cross that bridge when you get to it
That was the straw that broke the camel's back

"People usually live their lives mainly as the product of their conditioning and habits. The problem with this is.... your conditioning and habits create all kinds of limitations in your life; most of which you aren't fully aware of. Thus, you may be so accustomed to these limitations that you take them for granted and just accept and live with them; feeling that somehow there could be much more. That's because the basis of your conditioning and habits were caused by limitations when you were very young and not mentally developed to adapt; before you even learned how to talk."

Humbly submitted,

Tykeia Baker, Cousin

(Grand-daughter of the late Florence Speed,

Downtown Pat Brown's Closest Aunt)